2.ω

DAR TELLUM:
STRANGER FROM A DISTANT PLANET

DAR TELLUM:
STRANGER FROM A DISTANT PLANET

Written by JAMES R. BERRY
Illustrations by E. SCULL

Edited by ISAAC ASIMOV

WALKER AND COMPANY
New York

First published in the United States of America in
1973 by the Walker Publishing Company, Inc.

Published simultaneously in Canada by Fitzhenry
& Whiteside, Limited, Toronto.

Trade ISBN: 0-8027-6139-9
Reinf. ISBN: 0-8027-6140-2

Library of Congress Catalog Card Number: 72-95780

Printed in the United States of America.

10 9 8 7 6 5 4 3 2 1

To the many lower school children at St. Ann's whose comments helped shape this story; to Barry Dulany—librarian and storyteller—who read the story to several classes and contributed so many generous and important suggestions.

CONTENTS

Chapter 1

DAR TELLUM

They've called me a dreamer ever since I can remember. But maybe it's because I daydream a lot that I met Dar Tellum. I know I've met him, but I can't tell grown-ups. I've tried once or twice but all I got were funny looks. Once my mother felt my forehead. So I know they wouldn't believe the whole story.

That's why I'm writing this down for other kids to read. If I tell everything just the way it happened you'll believe me, even if it does sound pretty strange. And if the same thing ever happens to you, you'll know it's true even if no one else—especially grown-ups—

believes **you**.

So here it is.

I got the first hint of Dar Tellum about six months ago in old Mrs. Todd's class. She had just given us a long list of words. We were supposed to correct the ones not spelled right while she read something at her desk.

It was a clear, windy spring day and the blue sky was full of white, shiny clouds. I took one look out the window and forgot about the spelling words. At first, I wondered what it was like to be a cloud and float in air. Then I began wondering if a small fluffy cloud I saw was going to catch up to a larger one ahead of it.

That's when it came.

I felt a tug at my mind. You know how someone pokes you in line? Well, it was like getting poked. But inside my head. Then I heard words, like someone calling me. But too far away to make out well. And not out loud. The words were inside my head, too.

I thought real hard, trying to hear. I even forgot about the clouds and closed my eyes.

Then some words started to come more clearly, and I thought I heard: "Who are you?" I shut my mind to everything, and sort of saw something move inside it. I was beginning to see a kind of glow and to hear the words better.

Just then I felt Mrs. Todd beside me. I gulped hard and my heart began to pound as I looked up at her. She was staring down at me through her thick glasses, her mouth a thin, stern line in her face. She was really mad.

"Not one word corrected, Ralph Winston!" she snapped. "You'll do this list plus copying twenty more spelling words for extra homework. Now pay attention."

As she walked away I gave one last, quick look out the window (that small fluffy cloud was almost up to the big one by now) and tried to listen to Mrs. Todd the rest of the day. It was hard. I can't help it if I like daydreaming better than listening.

By the time I had had dinner and done the extra homework, I forgot about that tug at my mind. I just pushed it back with dozens of other things I can't explain yet. I didn't think I'd have that poke in my head or ever hear that voice again.

I was wrong. I met Dar Tellum again that night.

I was asleep. I know that. Then, there was that tug, just like in old Mrs. Todd's class. But strong enough to wake me up. I sat straight up in bed and felt the poke again, and heard someone call, as though he was talking through a long pipe. I was wide awake by now, and I squeezed my eyes tight together so I could think harder.

I saw a vague, hazy shape, like something through a window covered with mist from your breath. I tried to get closer to what it was. I sort of **thought** myself closer. Then two things happened.

The shape got a little bit clearer. Instead of just mist, I could see a fuzzy shape as tall as I am and thick and round.

And the voice got louder. In fact, loud enough so I could hear the words clearly.

Sometimes I get scared at night, especially after really weird dreams. But this time I wasn't. I just knew nothing bad would happen, and besides this wasn't a dream at all. I just didn't feel frightened.

The first thing I heard was: "Who are you?" Today when I look back I think the voice shook a bit, as if Dar Tellum were scared a little. I'm still not positive and he says he can't remember.

"I'm Ralph Winston. Who are you?" I answered right away. I didn't say the words out loud. I just thought them real hard. That seemed to work. There was a pretty long pause. Then:

"I am called Dar Tellum. This is very strange to me Ralph Winston."

I had never heard of a name like Dar Tellum before, but I didn't mention it just then. I remember thinking how softly he talked. And he had a funny kind of accent, too. But I still couldn't see him clearly. No matter how hard I tried he stayed a fuzzy, hazy shape.

"Ralph Winston, how is it that you can speak to me?" Dar Tellum asked. I had something to say then.

"You can just call me Ralph," I said inside my mind. No one ever calls me by my full name except Mrs. Todd, and that's only when she's mad. Then I added, "I don't know how I speak to you. How do you speak to me?"

"I do not know Ralph Win . . . I mean Ralph. Also, I cannot see you clearly. You look to me like a ball of fog."

So, Dar Tellum couldn't really see me either. That's when I guessed that both of us were going through the same thing for the first time.

I can't remember all the different things we talked about that night. Except one, something that Dar Tellum showed me that saved a lot of trouble later.

That came after I told him about baseball. Dar Tellum was puzzled.

"But Ralph, why hit a ball with a stick? You could make it move much more easily by telekinesis."

Long pause from me. Right. Now you're thinking the same thing that I did. What's that?

"Dar Tellum, what's tele . . . telekin . . . What's that you just said?" I asked.

"Ralph, telekinesis is . . . well . . . when I want to put something in a different place, I make it move by thinking it there."

"You think it there!" I was amazed. It was then that I wondered if maybe this was a dream after all. But only for a minute, because what came next showed me Dar Tellum knew what he was talking about. I calmed down and asked, "Could you teach me how to do it?"

"I believe it might be possible, Ralph," he

16

answered doubtfully. "If you wish we can try."

Then Dar Tellum told me what to do to try out tele . . . ah . . . telekinesis. (I still have trouble saying it. It should sound like tel-e-ke-nee'-sis.) I was supposed to look hard at an object, so hard that I felt its shape in my head. At that point, according to Dar Tellum, I could move what I was looking at.

"Can I try it right now?" I asked. Dar Tellum said that I could. He told me to use it on something small to begin with. It was dark outside, but still enough light came through the window for me to see a baseball on my desk. I looked at the ball and did what Dar Tellum had told me.

Nothing. The ball didn't move.

"Nothing happened, Dar Tellum. I guess I can't do it." I was really disappointed.

"Ralph, perhaps I can help you. Try again," he said.

So I stared at the baseball again and did what I was supposed to do. Then, I felt Dar Tellum helping me. It was like lifting a heavy package and someone comes along and carries one side. All of a sudden things feel half as heavy.

That's when I saw the ball move.

Very slowly it began to rise above my desk. And it stayed there. Then I made it move across the room. It floated over the floor until it was above my dresser. Then I put it down next to a model airplane I built a few months ago.

I couldn't believe it. I was so surprised that I couldn't say anything. I guess I got a little scared, but so would you if you had just seen what I saw. I breathed out and wiped sweat from my face. It was hard work moving that baseball by telekinesis.

Another thing I learned. Dar Tellum has to be around. I don't know why, but it won't work unless he helps.

I can't remember exactly what more we said that night. By the time we finished talking it was late and I was really tired. So tired that I couldn't think clearly—and that's why I didn't guess the truth about Dar Tellum until a whole day later.

I know that neither of us could figure out what was going on, or why, or if we'd see each other again. Dar Tellum was as puzzled about meeting me as I was about meeting him. We both felt that if this were a dream it was the most real dream we'd ever had. In fact, that night Dar Tellum and I agreed not to tell anybody just yet. No one would believe us. We could hardly believe it ourselves.

Chapter 2

CRISIS ON EARTH

The next thing I remember is Mom shaking me awake. "Get up, Ralph," I heard even though I was still half asleep, "you'll be late for school."

I finally kicked off the covers and put on my old blue jeans with a colored patch on the rear pocket and a striped shirt I really liked.

I was so tired as I dressed that morning that I almost forgot about Dar Tellum. With one arm in my shirt and the other arm out, I suddenly remembered. I just stood there, doing nothing for a moment.

Then I looked over at my dresser top. The

baseball sat there next to the model plane. Was all this real or not? I shook my head a couple of times wondering if last night was an extra real dream. What would you have thought? I just didn't know.

That is until Mrs. Todd's class in arithmetic. She gave us a long list of numbers to add and to multiply while she wrote a whole lot of homework on the board.

That's when it came again—that tug inside my head.

It's not easy to explain how it felt. But it was real. No dream could make me jerk up and start concentrating so hard. I couldn't tell how. But I knew Dar Tellum was trying to contact me.

So, when I felt that poke in my mind I tried real hard to make contact. My eyes squeezed together, my hands bunched up, and I thought as hard as I could. Dar Tellum's voice came closer and I saw a far away patch of some kind of hazy figure.

Because of what happened next I didn't get a chance to talk much to Dar Tellum just then. But all the excitement that followed proved one thing to me. He's as real as I am.

See, while I had my eyes closed contacting Dar Tellum, Mrs. Todd began walking beside the desks and checking the problems each of us were doing. Except me. I was really getting Dar Tellum's words clearly when just for a second I opened my eyes. There was Mrs. Todd, and only four desks away from mine.

Wow! Not one problem done, not one. And she could get as mad as I've ever seen a teacher get. And she doesn't mind giving a lot of extra homework either.

Then I thought of a way to get out of trouble. I squeezed my eyes shut and thought about as hard as I ever had.

"Dar Tellum, do you think we can do telekinesis now?" I asked. His voice came through clearly.

"If you wish, Ralph, we can try." I'll say this for Dar Tellum. He really acts fast. He didn't waste any time asking why, or just saying 'maybe.' I opened my eyes quickly. Mrs. Todd was only three desks from mine!

I saw a notebook on her desk. I did what

＠ＩＱＧＲＯ＠ＩＱＧＲＯ＠ＩＱＧＲＯ

Dar Tellum had told me to do with the baseball, but did it with the notebook. "Can you
help me now, Dar Tellum?" I asked quickly.
Mrs. Todd was only two desks away. It was
getting close.

Dar Tellum didn't say anything more, and
I think he kind of knew this was an emer-
gency. But suddenly I felt the notebook get
lighter and knew that he was helping. I took
a deep breath, held it, and put all my might
into making that notebook move. Then it
trembled and started to lift off Mrs. Todd's
desk. I clenched my hands harder with the
effort.

The notebook slowly rose above the desk,
as though it were floating in air. Then one of
the girls in the class noticed what was hap-
pening. I heard a kind of gasp, and then si-
lence. I guess other kids saw that notebook
just hanging in the air, too. Because I remember thinking how the class was quiet,
so quiet that you could hear Mrs. Todd walking to the desk in front of mine. And usually
she moves without hardly making a sound.

My idea was simply to tap Mrs. Todd with
the notebook and maybe take her attention

away from checking those problems I didn't do. But I was getting tired. And so was Dar Tellum. I could tell because the notebook was getting heavier and heavier. It took more and more work thinking just to keep it in the air.

So I gave one last big push with my mind. But I didn't have the control I thought I had, and the notebook flew forward faster than I expected. See, holding it above ground was the hardest part. It was easier making it move **through** the air. So it didn't just tap Mrs. Todd. It hit her in the back with a loud slap. Not so much it hurt. But enough to make her eyes grow wider and to gasp with surprise.

Just at the time the notebook moved toward Mrs. Todd one of the girls let out a loud scream. Then another. One of the guys in my class, his eyes wide and his mouth wide open, ran for the door and out of the classroom. Books fell, and other kids scrambled away from the notebook, which now was on the floor. In a second or two the whole class was either yelling or talking.

There was such an uproar that Mrs. Todd

forgot about checking those problems. By the time she got everyone quiet it was almost time to go home. She didn't give extra homework even, because she kind of half believed the story that everyone told her— about the notebook rising from her desk and flying through the air. She only told us to do the problems at home, which for me meant all of them.

I don't even remember when I broke contact with Dar Tellum, there was so much excitement. I remember thinking that I'd have to be more careful when we met. But I had proven one thing. Dar Tellum was no dream.

No use putting off homework. That's the first thing Mrs. Todd asks for when anyone comes into her room. She never forgets, just never. So when I was in bed that night, after saying good night to Mom and Dad, I got out the paper and did the arithmetic problems.

What came next changed everything.

When I was all through I got the idea of having some cookies and milk before going to sleep. At least a peanut butter and jelly sandwich if no cookies were around. After I

opened the door to my room I heard Dad
and Mom talking in the kitchen. And their
voices sounded so worried that I couldn't
help but sneak down the stairs and listen to
what they were saying.

First, I found out what my Dad really
does.

I knew he was some sort of an engineer,
but he never spoke much about his work at

28

home. It turned out that he was working on a secret government project and couldn't talk about his job to just anybody. You can bet I was curious. And it didn't take long to find out what the secret project was all about.

It seems that the planet Earth was right in the middle of a big crisis. Dozens of cities were in danger of becoming flooded. Already one city in some eastern country was almost covered with water. And the reason for this flooding was that the oceans were getting higher.

From what I understood, and I'm sure there are gaps here and there, the smoke from cars and factories goes into the air. When a part of this smoke called carbon dioxide gets into the atmosphere of Earth, it lets the sun's heat in. But it won't let much heat out. This carbon dioxide makes a kind of one way lid on Earth. Heat in, but not much out.

And this extra heat was warming up the north and south poles. So the ice was melting and the oceans were getting higher.

And that's where Dad came in.

He was working on a top secret government project to find ways to take this carbon dioxide out of the atmosphere, way up in the sky. But nothing seemed to work so far. That's why he was worried.

Thanks to Dar Tellum he did find a way, but that came later. Right then I forgot about getting a couple of cookies. Imagine, hundreds of cities under water unless Dad could find a way to take carbon dioxide out of the atmosphere.

I didn't know his job was so important.

It took a long time to get to sleep. I got so worried about the floods Earth might have that I even forgot about Dar Tellum.

But I met him again that night and got another surprise—one you've probably already guessed.

Let me tell you anyway.

Chapter 3

STRANGER FROM SIDRA

"Ralph, Ralph."

I was dreaming about giant cities flooded underwater. Dimly, I heard a voice calling me. It sounded hollow, like someone shouting down a long, long tunnel. Then I woke up, but I was still too sleepy to think clearly.

"Ralph, are you there?" a voice called in my mind. With a snap, I remembered Dar Tellum. I sat straight up.

"I'm here, Dar Tellum," I said out loud.

"Ralph, Ralph, can you hear me?" came Dar Tellum's voice again. He sounded disappointed now. I was going to answer out loud when I remembered something. I had

thought whatever I said to Dar Tellum before. Maybe he couldn't hear talking. So I squeezed my eyes shut and thought as loudly as I could.

"I'm here, Dar Tellum," I said, and at the same time I saw a fuzzy sort of glow. And this time he heard me.

"We broke contact quickly, Ralph. Did something go wrong?"

Dar Tellum meant the time in Mrs. Todd's class, right after that notebook hit her. So I told him what had happened and then he asked something strange. He asked what a class was.

How do you explain that to somebody? I did my best. Then he asked me something else that was even stranger. By now you've probably guessed what I should have caught on to. But I didn't, not until after Dar Tellum asked me what a school was.

How can you explain that? I had run out of explanations at this point. So I asked him, "Don't you go to school, Dar Tellum?" He took a few seconds to answer.

"There are nothing we call schools on Sidra, Ralph."

"Sidra! Where's Sidra?" I asked right away, thinking this was the name of a nearby city, or maybe one in another country where he lived. See, Dar Tellum and I had only really met just one night before. And so many things had happened that I never had time to wonder where he came from.

It turned out he lives on another planet somewhere in space, one that hasn't even been discovered yet!

"Ralph, Sidra is the name of my planet, the one with five moons circling a double sun, Candids. We're the fourth planet from Candids."

I couldn't believe it. My head buzzed and my stomach felt like a hollow ball. I had never even heard of anything like this before.

What's more, when I told Dar Tellum I lived on earth he was as surprised as I was. He hadn't ever heard of something like this either.

That night we talked over a lot of things, mostly wondering together how the two of us were able to contact each other, and if it had ever happened to anybody else before this.

Once we tried to get closer, to see each other more clearly.

It took work. I strained as hard as I could and so did Dar Tellum. Finally his hazy shape cleared a bit. I saw that he was a little taller than I am, and several wavy things came from his body that moved slowly up and down. But that's as clear as he became right then. He said I looked just as hazy to him, and we gave up trying.

Then, somehow, I began to tell Dar Tellum about Earth's crisis. At least as much as I remembered. When I finished he didn't say anything for a long time. I could almost sense how hard he was thinking. Finally he did speak.

"Ralph, I have an idea for your planet." And then he told me his plan.

I got into some trouble over his idea. But it worked, and from what I understand Dar Tellum's suggestion saved most of Earth from being covered with water. And the strange thing is how crazy his idea sounded at first.

ඥ෧෧෨෧෨෨෧෧ ඥ෧෨෨෧෨෧ ඥ෧෨෧ ෨෧෨෧

What Dar Tellum said was to put some tiny plants called algae into the atmosphere. He explained that some kinds of algae, which are plants so small you need a microscope to see each one, can live high up where it's cold. He said these plants would take carbon dioxide and turn it into oxygen. And, with carbon dioxide turned into oxygen, the Earth's heat could get out of the atmosphere, and the ice caps would stop melting.

Next we had to decide what kind of algae to use. I had a children's encyclopedia in my room and the article about algae named at least ten kinds. I read the names to Dar Tellum and he interrupted me when I came to one type. I could barely pronounce the name, but somehow he knew it would work best.

The idea of putting algae into the atmosphere was a simple idea. The logical person to tell was Dad. But how? I had to think about that. So I told Dar Tellum I'd contact him the next night and we said good-by. As soon as I let my mind relax he started to fade, just like steam from boiling water disappears in the air. Then, I was alone.

Sure I had an idea to save Earth. Great. Fine. Good. Swell. But how could I let Dad know about it? He'd want to hear how I got the idea and I'd have to tell him about Dar Tellum. He wouldn't believe me and he wouldn't like the idea after that.

I sat in bed, my head resting on my fist, thinking as hard as I could. Then it hit me. I had a way.

I wasn't going to tell Dad at all.

I remembered that he usually left his briefcase in the kitchen. Suppose I wrote out Dar Tellum's idea and just stuck it in his briefcase? He'd find it at work and no one would know I put it there. At least that's what I hoped.

I got out of bed and found some paper. Very carefully I printed out what Dar Tellum had told me, especially the kind of algae to use. Then I sneaked downstairs into the kitchen so quietly that only one stair creaked.

In the kitchen I made my mistake. I spotted some of my favorite cookies and instead of putting the note right into Dad's briefcase, I dropped it on the table and helped myself to the cookies and milk. I had finished what milk was left in the container and was still munching on one last cookie when I heard the stair creak. "Ralph, is that you down there?" Mom called out.

My heart jumped a few beats but I managed to gasp out a weak "Yes," while frantically looking around for a place to hide my note. If Mom ever saw it and began asking questions well . . . that would be the end of Dar Tellum's idea.

Then I saw a perfect hiding spot. Just as Mom's footsteps reached the door, I grabbed up the note and stuffed it inside the empty milk container. That's when the door swung back and Mom walked in.

"Are you all right, Ralph? I heard a noise and came down to see if it was you."

"Sure, Mom," I said, gulping hard to keep my voice from trembling. "I just wanted to get a bedtime snack." Then, from what Mom did next, I guessed that Dar Tellum's idea was gone, really gone.

"I'll clean up now, Ralph, you get to bed," Mom told me. Without any more warning,

she walked straight to the table and reached for the container.

Luckily for Earth I got a great idea. "I'll clean up, Mom. Really. I made a mess, I'll clean up," I said hurriedly. And before she could say anything else I grabbed up the container, stuck it in the refrigerator, and began rinsing my glass and plate. Mom just stood and stared at me.

"Well . . . I never thought. All right, I guess you're changing. But hurry up, there's school tomorrow," she said. Still looking surprised, Mom left.

When I heard the stair creak I knew she was almost to her room. I snatched the container out of the refrigerator and yanked out the note. Then, I opened the latches of Dad's briefcase and pushed the note into a file folder marked "New Proposals." That seemed to fit. Next, I finished rinsing the glass and plate, threw the container away, and got back to my room as fast as I could.

The idea was safe. In a few minutes I was fast asleep.

Chapter 4

THE ANSWER

Nothing happened for about a week.

During that time Dar Tellum and I contacted each other practically every night. We were getting to be really good friends by now, and I was learning more about how he lived.

One thing, for example. Dar Tellum doesn't go to school the way we do. I found this out when I asked him how he learned stuff like reading and writing.

"What's reading and writing, Ralph?" he asked me. I thought about how to tell him and did my best. But I still don't think he really understands what reading and writing is. Then I asked him how kids on Sidra learn things.

"By sharing from the fact colonies," he answered. It didn't make much sense to me, even though Dar Tellum tried to explain it. From the little I understood, these 'fact colonies' are a kind of school where Dar Tellum can get answers to questions he has. But he doesn't go there every day like we do.

Once I hit on something that still puzzles us. How does Dar Tellum speak English? People on another planet wouldn't speak any Earth language. The next time we contacted each other I asked Dar Tellum where he learned English. Was he surprised.

"Ralph, we are not speaking English. We are talking in the Sidran language. I have wondered about this, too."

"It sounds like English to me, Dar Tellum," I told him.

We talked it over and that's when we learned that my words came out in his language, Sidran. And when he spoke to me his words turned out in English. But the way they came out wasn't perfect and that's why he has an accent.

Dar Tellum told me I had an accent in Sidran. He hinted once that it was a bad accent, too. But it was only a hint. Dar Tellum is always pretty polite.

One thing we tried was to see each other better. We had practiced making contact a lot and by now it was easy—even during the day when there were lots of things to distract us. But somehow we still found it hard to see each other clearly. Then one night we made a special effort.

I thought as hard as I could and so did Dar Tellum. The fuzzy kind of mist that was usually between us started to go away. I strained even harder.

Then I saw a shape about my size, but thicker. The shape was surrounded by what looked like large, flat paddles that moved

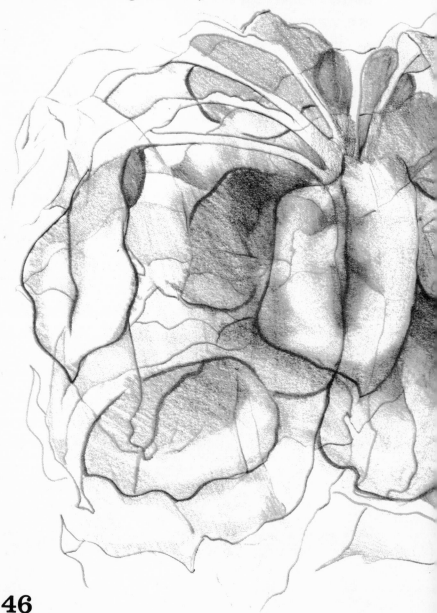

slowly up and down. But I can't be sure how because as soon as I stopped thinking with all my might, the mist and haze rolled back.

ᘓᕲ ᘌᕬᕼ ᘓᕲ ᘌᕬᕼ ᘓᕲ ᘌᕬᕼ

We were so tired from all the effort of pushing back that mist that we had to break contact that night.

The fact I was staying up pretty late talking to Dar Tellum must have showed.

"Ralph, you really look tired," Mom mentioned one morning. That's when I made a big mistake. See, I wanted to tell Mom and Dad about Dar Tellum. After you make a new friend or something exciting happens it's only natural. But it **was** a mistake.

"Mom, I guess I am. It's sort of . . . well . . . that I'm visiting with someone every night," I said eagerly. Mom shot a worried look at me. Her eyes widened, and she kept staring at me so I felt as though I had to go on.

"Well, you see . . . this friend of mine and me, we sort of get together. He's from another planet and . . . I think he is anyhow."

By this time I was stumbling along, trying to make it sound better and getting more confused by the second. That's when Mom felt my forehead. I stopped right then. It

48

wasn't going to work. I shouldn't have tried. At that moment, I made up my mind never to mention Dar Tellum to anybody, at least not grown-ups. They wouldn't believe a word of it.

I'm glad I figured things out. Because otherwise I might have told Dad about Dar Tellum that night. And the way things turned out it would have been a bigger mistake.

See, as soon as Dad came home I knew something was wrong. He gave me a queer look, half mad and half anxious. But he didn't say anything until after dinner.

"Ralph, I'd like to talk to you." When you hear those words you know something's coming. Dad led me into the living room.

"Anything important, Dad?" I asked, being as carefree as I could. It didn't work and I felt like someone who's just been given a year's supply of homework.

Dad got straight to the point.

"Ralph, did you ever put anything in my briefcase?" That's all he said, too, but I knew he meant business. I gulped hard and stared at a shiny spot on one of my shoe tips.

"WELL!"

I knew I better say something soon.

"Ugg . . . errr . . . just once, Dad," I managed to mutter, feeling pretty scared. Then I decided I better tell him something. But leaving out Dar Tellum. I wasn't going to change my mind about that.

"Dad, I got this idea in a dream. And I knew it might help so I wrote it out and put it in your briefcase. Did you get into trouble, Dad?" I asked as I looked up.

"No, Ralph, no trouble. Some scientists I work with tested the idea about shooting algae into the atmosphere," he said. "From what they tell me the idea will work. In fact it's the only one we found that might save Earth's cities. I think you'll be visited by an important person soon. And he'll want to know how you got your idea," he added, looking at me in a funny kind of way.

At that moment I realized that Dad suspected something more than what I told him. I felt I had to say something.

"Eh, well Dad, probably the old family genius at work, huh?" I said cheerily while forcing out a chuckle. Dad didn't laugh. In fact he just kept looking at me. He really was suspicious.

I got out of the room as fast as I could. It wasn't until I was almost in bed that I realized the important thing. Dar Tellum's idea would probably save Earth.

Suddenly I was very happy.

Chapter 5

ROCKET LAUNCHING

Dar Tellum had the right idea all right. But without still more of his help it wouldn't have worked. I'll tell the story as it happened.

The next week passed quickly, with Dar Tellum and I contacting each other at least once a day. Then one afternoon when I got home from school I found my father and another man waiting for me.

"Ralph, this is Dr. Wheeler, from the office where I work," Dad said. I nodded my head and said hello, wondering what was up, sort of trying to see if this meant trouble or not. It didn't. He seemed nice, not half so scary as I had imagined when Dad said he might come.

"Ralph, I was wondering how you got the idea about sending algae into the atmosphere," Dr. Wheeler said.

"Here we go again," I thought to myself. If I told him about Dar Tellum he'd think I was crazy.

"Well . . . ah . . . it just came in a dream. But a really real dream. That's about all, Dr. Wheeler," I stuttered.

Dr. Wheeler and Dad looked at me and I knew they didn't know what to think. "Another reason I came, Ralph," said Dr. Wheeler, "is to invite you to the launching of the first rocket that will carry this algae into the atmosphere."

WOW! A chance to see a rocket launching. I shouted, "Sure," and got so excited that they started smiling. Then they told me the launching was planned for tomorrow. A school day. Nothing could be more perfect.

That night I contacted Dar Tellum as soon as I could. By now we could do it instantly, just by thinking hard in a certain way. When we did, I told him I was going to see a rocket launching.

"What's a launching, a rocket launching?" he asked. That stumped me for a few seconds.

"Don't you have rockets on Sidra?" I asked in return.

"What are rockets, Ralph?" Dar Tellum answered. I knew by now this was typical. Once Dar Tellum wanted to know something he just kept on asking about it. If I asked a question in return he'd just ignore it and ask one of his own. That's the way they did it on Sidra.

I told Dar Tellum all I knew about rockets and how they work and what they do, like bringing men to the moon and back. When I finished, Dar Tellum seemed to be thinking for a long time.

"It seems a wonderful thing, Ralph, to visit your moon. It's all very strange to me. We on Sidra live in a completely different way," he said in a lonely sort of voice. Just then, for a moment, I wondered if it would be possible for Dar Tellum to visit Earth. Or, better yet, for me to visit Sidra. But I didn't wonder too long because I was tired and after talking a few more minutes we broke contact and I went to sleep, thinking about tomorrow.

"Hurry up, Ralph. You don't want to be late," was the next thing I heard. Someone was shoving me gently by the shoulder. Dad. Wearily I opened my eyes. The launching!

Once I remembered that, I didn't have any trouble waking up, even if it was still dark outside. Mom had breakfast waiting for us by the time I got downstairs, and soon Dad and I were in a car heading for the launching site. After an hour or so we arrived. Practically nothing was around except some cement buildings. And the rocket, of course.

It was tall, thin, and silvery. The dawn was breaking by now and the tip of the rocket glistened from early sunlight. There wasn't even a small breeze, and I could hear crickets chirping. Then I saw Dr. Wheeler along with lots of other people. We entered one of the buildings, launching headquarters, Dad called it, and went to a large glass window that looked into a big, white room.

꿍꿍 ꒰꒰ 꿍꿍 ꒰꒰꒰ 꿍꿍 ꒰꒰ 꿍꿍

"That's where we grew the algae, Ralph," Dr. Wheeler told me. A man in a white coat was in the room closing a tall square box that looked something like a container of milk. Next to it was another box that looked just like it.

"The room is sealed so that germs from outside can't get in to spoil the algae," Dr. Wheeler explained. "Right now we're filling the container with algae. From this room it will be put into the rocket and shot into the atmosphere."

Then he spoke to my Dad. I can't remember exactly every word. But it's a lucky thing I was there to contact Dar Tellum.

See, it seems that some scientists weren't sure that the type of algae Dar Tellum named would work. So they grew another kind, too. And right on the table in the big room were both kinds—each kind in one of those containers.

Dr. Wheeler told my Dad that they had made some tests just the night before and had picked one type of algae to be shot into the air. **But not the kind that Dar Tellum named.** My Dad shook his head, and I could tell he wasn't happy about the choice.

Then I had a suggestion.

"Why not put both types into the air?" I said. They all looked at me, and Dad answered.

"Because if the experiment was a success we wouldn't know which kind of algae was best. We'd have to waste time growing both, and time is too short for that."

Right then I decided to check with Dar Tellum. It's a lucky thing for Earth that I did.

The others were talking about the launching and not paying attention to me. I closed my eyes. "Dar Tellum, can you contact me now?" I called out in my mind. Dar Tellum answered right away.

"Yes, Ralph, I can hear you."

I didn't waste any time. I told him the name of the kind of algae they were going to shoot in the upper atmosphere. Dar Tellum sounded as excited as I've ever heard him.

"That is the wrong type, Ralph. It won't work well. I know."

At that moment, the only thing on my mind was how to switch containers.

I'll bet you have the same idea as I had.

Telekinesis. I asked Dar Tellum if he'd help. Those containers looked kind of heavy, but he was willing to try.

The man in the white coat had put a container in a small tray and then left the room for a moment. I guessed that container was the one about to go in the rocket. If I was going to switch them, now was the time. If I didn't, the experiment would fail and cities around the world would be flooded before anyone saw the mistake.

I clenched my hands together and Dar Tellum and I began telekinesis. The container on the tray was heavy. Both of us strained with all our might before I even felt it move. Luckily we only had to lift it an inch or so to clear the edge of the tray.

Sweat dripped down my back. My head hurt from the strain. My hands ached. But then I finally felt the container lift.

Quickly I made it move right beside the other one.

Next—move the other container with the correct kind of algae into the tray. But I was tired. Real tired. So was Dar Tellum. It's a lot of work doing telekinesis.

ᘿᓂᓄ ᘒᘓᘔ ᘿᓂᓄ ᘒᘓᘔ ᘿᓂᓄ ᘒᘓᘔ

We strained hard but barely made the container move upwards. But we could slide it, and that's exactly what we did. It skidded slowly across the table, Dar Tellum and I getting more tired by the second. It reached the edge of the tray. We tried a last effort to lift it on.

No good. We couldn't make it move, much less lift it up. Then the man in the white coat came back into the room and walked right toward the tray.

I figured we had lost. We had come so close to winning that I almost felt like crying. I watched the man in the white coat get closer to the tray, as disappointed as I ever have been. But he only stared at it for a second or so. Then he slowly shook his head from side to side, looking first at one container then at the other.

Just then Dr. Wheeler called in through an intercom system, saying that everybody was waiting. I guess that decided which container went up in the rocket. Because the man in the white coat **picked up the container Dar Tellum and I had moved and put it in the tray.** Then he carried the tray out of the room. It was pure luck that he didn't double check the markings on those containers. Just luck.

It didn't take long to put the algae into the rocket. In a half hour they began the countdown. I looked at the launching through another window in the building. When they reached "zero" I heard a roar.

Red fire came from the rocket's tail, like hot clouds. Then it rose, slowly at first, but gaining speed all the time.

The rocket turned a red silvery color when it went high enough for the sun to shine on it more. Then it gradually disappeared into the sky, getting smaller all the time. The last thing I saw of the rocket was the red exhaust from its tail, small as a pinpoint, against the sky.

That night I contacted Dar Tellum when I reached my room.

CRICRICRICRICRICRI

"I think it will be a success, Ralph. I'm sure the algae in the atmosphere will soon cure your planet of its troubles," Dar Tellum said.

Dar Tellum was right. A month or so later Dad told me that many more rockets around the world were being sent into the atmosphere with loads of algae. By the time they had found out the wrong container— but really the right one—was in that rocket it was too late. Then they found that the algae they did shoot up turned carbon dioxide back into oxygen faster than anyone expected. They used the kind Dar Tellum said from then on. Earth's crisis was over.

Now I realize how Dar Tellum figured out which algae to use because I soon got to know him a lot better. I'll tell you about that sometime, including my visit to Sidra. But I've written this down so you know Dar Tellum is real and how his idea saved Earth, and how it almost didn't work.

Don't bother telling any grown-ups about him because they won't believe you. And if you ever meet Dar Tellum yourself, or a friend of his, I can tell you another thing for certain.

Keep it a secret.

The End